Johnny Appleseed Gets His Name

Glooscap Makes the Seasons

Two American Tall Tales

retold by Cynthia Swain

illustrated by Karen Leon and George Almond

Table of Contents

TALL TALES

What is a tall tale?

A tall tale is an imaginative and usually funny story in which some details and actions are greatly exaggerated, or overstated. Tall tales often feature a hero or heroine who is based on a real person, but he or she becomes larger than life in the stories. The hero is often bigger, stronger, more skillful, and more courageous than an ordinary person.

What is the purpose of a tall tale?

A tall tale entertains people and teaches about good character traits. The hero shows strength, wit, determination, and courage over great odds. A tall tale often shows how human strength, cleverness, and know-how can overcome nature, machines, or just plain evil. The hero or heroine solves problems and beats out bullies in fun ways.

How do you read a tall tale?

The title usually names the hero or heroine. The beginning of the story often tells about the hero's special abilities. Then the author will introduce the problem of the story or the "bully." Ask yourself, "How will the main character use his or her powers to defeat this bad guy?" Then get ready to be amused and surprised.

Features of a Tall Tale

A tall tale is usually a funny story with exaggerations.

The main character is a hero or heroine and often is based on a real person.

The hero may have a helper that might be an animal or object.

The hero has superhuman strength and skills.

The hero has to fight or outwit a "bully" in the form of nature, an animal, a machine, or a group of people.

Who invented tall tales?

Many tall tales can be traced back to the 1800s and are set on the American frontier. The brave settlers of these areas faced rough land, raging rivers, terrible storms, wild animals, and "bad guys." People made up tales about heroes and heroines with superhuman powers to help them cope with their difficult lives. The tall tales made people laugh and gave them courage to face their problems and overcome the challenges that lay before them.

3

The Origins of Two Tall Tales

Johnny Appleseed, a Tall Tale from Ohio: Johnny Appleseed's real name was John Chapman. He was born on September 26, 1774, in Leominster, Massachusetts. When he grew up, he owned tree farms in Ohio, Pennsylvania, Kentucky, Illinois, and Indiana. Some of his apple trees still produce apples today.

Johnny was a kind man. Since he was friends with both the pioneers and the Native Americans, he often helped settle problems between the two groups. Johnny's wish was that no one would ever go hungry. He died in 1845 at the age of seventy. People celebrate his life with a yearly Appleseed Festival in the city where he is buried— Fort Wayne, Indiana.

Johnny Appleseed was a real-life person who spent fifty years growing apple trees in the midwestern United States.

4

Glooscap, a Tall Tale from Maine: Glooscap was the mythical hero of the Wabanaki (wah-buh-NAH-kee) Indians and other tribes who lived on the eastern seaboard of what are now the United States and Canada. It is said that Glooscap created the animals, the first people, and many natural features such as mountains, rivers, and islands.

In different legends, Glooscap's name is spelled different ways, such as *Gluskabe* and *Kloskomba*.

Many Native Americans believed that Glooscap was their creator and protector.

Tools Writers Use
Metaphor

A **metaphor** (MEH-tuh-for) compares two things that are alike in one way. Metaphors directly describe something by using the word **is** or **was** rather than **like** or **as**. For example: "The baby's happiness was a hug from mommy." Authors use metaphors to help readers create pictures in their minds. Notice how the author of these tales uses this type of comparison to describe what something feels, looks, tastes, smells, sounds, or acts like. Authors also use metaphors to show how characters or objects resemble or represent something else.

Johnny Appleseed Gets His Name

There once was a boy named John Chapman. He lived on a farm with his parents in New England. His favorite job was to **tend** the trees in the apple orchard. He took good care of each and every tree. As a result, red, green, and golden apples that were big and tasty grew everywhere.

Creatures big and small visited and played with Johnny. They loved him because he had the heart of a bear but was as gentle as a lamb. People loved Johnny, too. He was a friendly sort, even if he was a bit odd.

For one thing, Johnny never wore shoes. He said his feet always felt hot! In the spring and summer, he liked the way the grass tickled his toes. In the fall and winter, he liked the way the mud and snow felt on his bare feet. Because he never wore shoes, the bottoms of his feet were as tough as an elephant's hide. Secondly, Johnny never wanted to leave the orchard, even at night. The soft soil was his bed and the leaves were his blanket. Johnny was at home outdoors.

"Johnny," his mother would say, "come home and sleep in your bed. You can't stay outside all the time. You're not some type of animal who lives in the woods."

"I love the apple orchard too much to come inside, Mother. One day, I'll visit every orchard in the country—even the ones out west," said Johnny.

"Johnny, there aren't any apples in the West, just fields of corn and wheat!" said his mother.

When Johnny heard that, a big lightbulb turned on in his head. "No apples in the West? Now that is a crying shame. I'll make it my business to bring apples to the West," said the **steadfast** Johnny. He was determined to fulfill his goal.

The winter after he turned eighteen, Johnny left home. He made a coat out of an old sack. For a hat, he wore a tin pot that could also be used for cooking. Last, he grabbed a bag of apple seeds and went on his way. John Chapman was a strange sight to behold, but he didn't care how he looked. The whole country would be his garden. He would find new places to **sow**, or plant, his apple seeds.

Johnny walked from town to town and from state to state. Each night he camped out under the stars and cooked using his pot. When the ground was frozen and there was no water to drink, he used his hot heels to melt the snow. He planted apple orchards everywhere he went. Eventually, he planted orchards from Pennsylvania to the Great Plains.

One day in early spring, he spotted a beautiful clearing in the Ohio River Valley. He began to plant seeds and young trees. When people heard about the strange-looking man, they came out to watch him. Many **snickered** at Johnny. Some laughed at what he was doing. Others laughed at the way he dressed.

"What are you up to, fool?" said one farmer. "You look like a clown in that old sack. You should be planting corn or wheat like us. Who needs apples?"

Johnny said nothing. He knew that many people in the West had never tasted apples. They didn't know that apples made a **zesty** cider that was sharp and sweet. They had never eaten a piece of apple pie.

When it was harvest time, people watched Johnny pick his apples. He took the first one and walked over to the farmer who had called him a fool.

"Please accept this as my gift to you," Johnny said as he handed the juicy apple to the farmer.

The farmer was afraid to eat the apple, but Johnny **encouraged** him. He urged him to at least try it.

The farmer took a small bite. Then he quickly took another and another. The flavor was a party for his taste buds! In a minute, he had gobbled up the entire apple.

"How was it?" Johnny asked.

"Delicious!" answered the farmer. "May I have another?" All the people gathered around Johnny and begged to try his apples. They loved every last bite.

"I shouldn't have called you a fool," **lamented** the farmer. He was sorry for what he had said. "We should honor you. From now on, we'll call you Johnny Appleseed."

And that's how Johnny Appleseed got his name.

Reread the Tall Tale

Analyze the Characters and Plot
- Who were the characters in the tall tale?
- Which character was the hero? How do you know?
- Who tried to discourage the hero?
- How did the hero deal with these people?

Analyze the Tools Writers Use: Metaphor
Find examples of metaphors in the tale.
- What did the author say the soil and leaves were? (page 7) How are these things like the objects that the author compares them to?
- What did the author mean by saying "a lightbulb turned on" in Johnny's head? (page 8)
- What caused the farmer to have "a party for his taste buds"? (page 11)

Focus on Words: Direct Definitions
Authors often define words directly in the text. Sometimes the definition comes after a comma and the word **or**. Other times, the definition occurs in other places in the sentence or even in the next sentence. Make a chart like the one below. Then reread the tall tale to find direct definitions for the following story words.

Page	Word	Definition in Text
7	tend	
8	steadfast	
8	sow	
9	snickered	
10	zesty	
11	encouraged	
12	lamented	

Glooscap Makes the Seasons

A long, long time ago, a mighty tribe lived in the North Country. They lived in peace and harmony with the land. Glooscap was their spirit and protector. He guided them and looked after them.

Glooscap was the mightiest spirit that ever walked the earth or flew in the sky. He was stronger than a thousand men. He was wiser than ten thousand men. When he slept, he was the size of a million men. Maine was his bed and Nova Scotia his pillow.

One year, the North Country was so cold that the ice and snow couldn't melt. The people weren't able to grow their corn. It was too cold to hunt.

"Glooscap," the people called, "please help us. We will **perish** from **famine**." The people were in danger of dying because there was nothing to eat.

Glooscap **pledged** to help. He promised to make things right for his people. He would go on a journey and speak to the giant, Winter. Winter was a cunning and hateful giant who **despised** every living thing. He had an icicle for a heart.

The author introduces the setting in the beginning of the story so the reader knows where the story takes place. The setting is a key element in this story.

The author uses metaphors to describe Glooscap's great size and strength. Exaggerations like these help the reader create a fun mental picture and are a typical feature of a tall tale.

Here the author introduces the problem of the story and shows that Glooscap is heroic. This is the mark of a tall tale hero. We read on to find out if Glooscap will solve the problem.

Finally, Glooscap arrived at Winter's ice palace. The giant pretended to be friendly. He acted like a nice host and gave Glooscap food and drink.

What Glooscap did not know was that the drink had magical powers. It put Glooscap into a deep sleep. Time seemed to stand still. A month later, Glooscap awoke. By then, Winter had left for the Far North Country.

The author brings in a "bad guy," a bully in the character of Winter. He is going to be a tough opponent for Glooscap. That is a good way to get the reader to care about, and root for, the hero.

"Alas," cried Glooscap. "I have been tricked by Winter. My people will die from the cold. What shall I do?"

Then Glooscap heard a sweet song. It was music to his ears. He looked over to the ocean and saw a giant whale.

"I travel both north and south every year," sang the whale. "Come with me and I will take you to Summer. She is all heart and will help you."

A singing, talking whale adds some fun, or whimsy, to the story. She is the tall tale hero's helper, or "sidekick."

Glooscap thanked the whale for her kindness and climbed onto her back for a ride. Each day of their journey south grew warmer and warmer. When they finally came to land, Glooscap stepped off the whale. He went looking for Summer.

Glooscap found Summer at the foot of a mountain. She wore a crown made from flowers and twigs. She danced merrily around the woods with her lovely daughters.

Wherever they went, bright sunshine followed. Everything Summer passed grew green and full.

Glooscap called out to Summer, "Please help my people. The North Country is dying from the cold. We need your special powers to bring life back to the land."

Summer was a wise and good giant. She called for her gentle breezes to be a chariot. They rode a rainbow to the North Country. When Glooscap arrived with Summer, the ice and snow began to melt.

Winter saw what was happening and grew angry. Summer was his enemy. He hated her. Winter called forth all of his powers and said, "Go away! I **banish** the sun!" Winter told the sun to leave, but it refused. Then Winter made a blizzard. Cold winds whipped across the land. But the sun beamed even more. The blizzard soon turned into a warm spring shower.

The author has Winter and Summer, who are enemies, face each other. This adds action to the story, which keeps the reader's interest. Plus, if Winter wins, that means the problem will get worse!

The first stalks of corn pushed their tiny green heads through the ground. Birds could be heard singing their sweet songs.

"You have beaten me, Summer," sighed Winter. "The people do not want me around. I will go away from here forever. But where can I go?" Winter felt helpless and ashamed for all that he had done.

Summer and her daughters smiled sweetly. They would be happy to be with the people all year round.

Then Glooscap saw icy tears skate down Winter's cheeks. Glooscap knew that the people did not like Winter when he was mean. But Glooscap also knew that the people needed Winter. Winter gave people time to rest from long days in the fields, time to make new things, and more time to read and think.

Glooscap talked to Summer in private. She nodded her head. Then Glooscap told Winter his idea. "You can stay here for six months each year," proclaimed Glooscap. "But *only* for six months. You must go to the Far North Country for the rest of the year."

"And what about her?" asked Winter anxiously.

"When you leave, Summer will take your place. Then the people will have all the sunshine they need. In the six months with Summer, they can grow their crops, hunt for food, and plan for your return."

The author shows that tall tale heroes often use their brains. Glooscap uses his wisdom to solve the problem in a fair way.

Winter looked at Glooscap. He looked at Summer. Then he looked at the people. Finally, Winter nodded his head in agreement. Then he flew away on a crisp gust of wind.

And that is how Glooscap made the seasons.

Reread the Tall Tale

Analyze the Characters and Plot
- Who were the characters in the tall tale?
- Which character was the hero? How do you know?
- Who was the bully? How did the hero deal with the bully?
- Who helped the hero? Would you consider her a heroine? Why or why not?

Analyze the Tools Writers Use: Metaphor
What does the author mean when . . .
- Glooscap's bed and pillow are described as "Maine and Nova Scotia"? (page 15)
- she calls Winter's heart "an icicle"? (page 15)
- the whale describes Summer as "all heart"? (page 17)

Focus on Words: Direct Definitions
Make a chart like the one below. Then reread the tall tale to find direct definitions for the following story words.

Page	Word	Definition in Text
15	perish	
15	famine	
15	pledged	
15	despised	
18	banish	

How does an author write a
TALL TALE?

Reread "Glooscap Makes the Seasons" and think about what the author did to write this tall tale. How did she develop the story? How can you, as a writer, develop your own tall tale?

 1.

Decide on a Hero

Remember, a tall tale has a hero or heroine who uses strength and skills to solve a problem. In "Glooscap Makes the Seasons," the author wanted to show how a determined protector could help his people.

 2.

Brainstorm Characters
Writers ask these questions:

- What kind of hero is my main character? What special abilities does my main character have?
- How does my main character use these abilities? What does he or she do, say, or think?
- Does anyone help the main character solve a problem? What special abilities does this character have?
- Who will be the bully or bullies in the story? How will these characters challenge the hero?

Characters	Traits	Actions Based on Traits
Glooscap	brave; concerned	determined to help his tribe no matter what
Winter	tricky; hateful	didn't want anything to live
Summer	kind; wise	helped Glooscap get a warm season for growing crops

3. Brainstorm Setting and Plot

Writers ask these questions:

- Where does my tall tale take place? When does it take place? How will I describe the place and time?
- What is the problem, or situation?
- How does the hero or heroine solve the problem?
- How does the tall tale end?
- How does the story use exaggeration to add humor and highlight the most important parts?

Setting	long, long ago in the North Country
Problem of the Story	The weather is so cold that people cannot grow food or hunt.
Story Events	1. Glooscap tries to talk to Winter, but Winter tricks him and escapes. 2. A friendly whale takes Glooscap to Summer. 3. Summer goes to the North Country with Glooscap.
Solution to the Problem	Glooscap has Summer and Winter agree to share the North Country—six months of cold weather and six months of warm weather.

Glossary

banish   (BA-nish) to make someone leave a place (page 18)

despised   (di-SPIZED) hated; considered unworthy of attention (page 15)

encouraged   (in-KER-ijd) inspired with courage and hope; helped (page 11)

famine   (FA-min) a severe shortage of food (page 15)

lamented   (luh-MEN-ted) expressed sadness or regret (page 12)

perish   (PAIR-ish) to die (page 15)

pledged   (PLEJD) promised (page 15)

snickered   (SNIH-kerd) laughed while trying not to be heard doing so (page 9)

sow   (SOH) to plant seeds, often by scattering (page 8)

steadfast   (STED-fast) determined (page 8)

tend   (TEND) to take care of (page 7)

zesty   (ZES-tee) full of flavor (page 10)